Embrace

Riverton Cove Series

Renee Field

Embrace

Riverton Cove series, Book I

Sweet romance novella
By Renee Field

EMBRACE

First edition. February 21, 2014.

Copyright © 2014 Renee Field.

ISBN: 978-1393321897

Written by Renee Field.

Dedication to all the women looking for a second chance at love. I say jump for it!

All the mistakes in this novella are my own.

Embrace
By Renee Field

Ella O'Connor left her small rural town of Cape Cod for the big Apple and never looked back. Now that she's made a career in New York she knows something is missing. A frantic call from her sister has her leaving everything behind, including her finance, as she makes her way home fearing the worst for her mother. Being home opens old feelings she thought long dead.

A winter storm forces Ella off the road and who saves her but the one man she'd prayed to never see again.

Paul Carter can't believe his eyes when he spots his old high school flame in the silly mini-car that should be banned from Cape Cod roads in winter. Rescuing her ignites desires he tried to bury. Divorced and now a successful business man, he vows not to get swayed by the cute brunette with the shapely bottom, and hips that would make a saint weep. Within a week though it seems everywhere he goes Ella is there and every time he sees her he wants her more.

Can two people who started out whispering high school dreams to each other embrace the opportunity to rediscover the meaning of love?

Chapter One

Ella thought for the second time that day she should have rented an SUV. The small, compact car had called to her in the rental parking lot but about thirty minutes outside of the Newport State Airport the snow had started to fall and she'd cursed going with her feminine instinct which had screamed 'Pick the cute Mini'. She slowed down and cranked up the radio and tried hard to not think about why she had gone on impulse control to begin with, and failed.

Her sister's frantic call to her last night had rocked Ella's world. For the first time in five years Ella had cancelled her heavy work schedule and booked a flight home ASAP. At five in the morning she'd hailed a taxi in the ever-constant New York traffic to take her to JFK to supposedly hop on a short flight to Barnstable Municipal Airport which the locals called the Hyannis Airport. Things hadn't gone as planned. Her flight had been delayed because of technical difficulties which meant a five hour wait at JFK. By the time the plane landed in Hyannis and after she'd dealt with the rental agency she had texted her sister informing her she'd make her own way home. Plus she didn't want her sister to leave their mother alone in the hospital.

The radio had played a constant litany of love songs since the moment she'd turned it on. While she'd like to switch the channel, navigating getting off the ramp from the highway to the smaller road required her immediate attention. The snow had packed about five inches down already and what the weather man had called a few flurries was becoming what she knew in her bones to be an incoming blizzard. That was the thing about Newport. It had its own weather system that mystified the meteorologists in the Big Apple. Gripping the wheel, all Ella wanted to do was get to her family homestead in one piece. Seriously though, if she heard another heartache song she might totally fall apart.

Ella forced the car to a crawl as the Mini's tires sought traction and breathed a sigh of relief when she spotted the highway sign for

Route 6. A road she knew like the back of her hand. Passing through the familiar landscape brought another rush of memories Ella didn't want to examine. She'd left and hadn't looked back but that didn't mean there weren't times when living in New York, with its constant noise and people didn't get to her. Turning left onto a secondary road, she bypassed the rich area of Newport known for its showy magazine-ready mansions and tourist haunts and settled in for another forty-five minutes of driving.

Her last text from her sister had said they'd released their mother from the hospital which had surprised Ella. *Was that normal?* According to her sister Tara, it had been a minor stroke and the hospital couldn't do anything else for her, plus their demanding mother was insisting on going home. That had sounded like her mother and for once it made Ella smile. Demanding to a fault, she was also loving and it had been her mother's determination that had enabled Ella to leave the small town of Riverton to pursue a law degree. Even after the sudden death of her father, Ella's mother didn't slow down or expect her daughters to do anything but pursue their dreams.

That however didn't explain why she had avoided coming home for close to five years. The truth of the matter was that the last time she'd been home she'd heard her high school sweetheart, Paul Carter, had gotten engaged. The thought of seeing him with someone else had been enough to fortify her heart that the best course of action would be staying away. While she might admit to herself she was being a chicken, that didn't mean she'd openly let on how much she wished things had been different.

When Love You Always, another Lionel Richie top 40 song started to play on the radio, Ella had enough. Flicking stations, she sought a Christmas song and sighed heavily when she couldn't find one. Christmas songs it seemed were only in fashion on December 24th through to the 26th, and with it only being the 15th of the month she'd have to wait two more weeks for her favorite jingles. At least her mother would be playing them because Christmas, like most holidays in the O'Connor home, was to be celebrated with music, food and more food.

A pang of longing hit Ella when she realized that while she'd stayed away for five years, she'd actually missed more than a dozen Christmas gatherings with her family and that damn feeling of guilt eased into her. While some of her excuses had been legitimate because law school was not for the faint of heart, the truth had been it was easier to stay away. Going home always made her want to stay and she'd promised herself she'd never live in a small town, where everyone knew your name and your business when they shouldn't. But was living in a big city any better? That had been the question haunting her lately. Everything about New York was starting to grate on her nerves. From the constant honking of the taxis, to the sour-ripe smell of the city that permeated the air all year but got constantly worse as the weather heated up for summer, she was beginning to question if living in the big city was worth it.

To those from her small town, she'd made it. Over the last few years she'd tried telling herself that meant something, but knowing her mother was getting older and that she'd basically abandoned her sister, making it didn't sound so good or make her feel great. Sure she'd left the small rural town behind and now had a solid reputation as a good real estate lawyer with a medium-sized firm but if Ella looked at her life for any length of time she'd find it wanting. She worked long hours, and when not working she hit the fitness center. Her apartment cost more than her mother had made in a year and while she'd looked at a number of condos recently she couldn't seem to purchase a place. Nothing called to her, or so she told herself.

She passed Beckman's old farm, slowing down more to take a good look at the place. The farm looked deserted and Ella didn't like how that made her feel. Mary Beckman had been a good friend to the O'Connor family and growing up Ella had enjoyed helping out on the farm. She wondered what had happened. Mary had two sons and Ella thought for sure they'd follow in the family footsteps and stay close to home. Guess she had been wrong. Change happened to all families but the thought of her old family house, which had been passed down for a hundred years falling to decay filled her heart with angst.

Turning the corner, she fought with the wheel a little too hard and cursed yet again she'd taken the Mini Cooper over the SUV. This time the tires couldn't find traction and pumping the brake only made the car spin wildly out of control. Ella's last thought as the car hit the embankment was that next time, she'd ignore her feminine impulses and think more like the lawyer she was known for—rational to a fault.

Chapter Two

Paul had been tailing the slow to a fault driver for a good thirty miles and he'd cursed enough time that had his father been alive and in the truck, he'd actually for once in his life be proud of him. After all his father's regular vocabulary had been sailor-talk, where every second word consisted of an expletive. Thankful at least his father was long dead and buried, Paul forced his mind to the present. The snow was picking up and the satellite had shown a Nor'easter coming, not that the stupid weather man from New York on the radio channels once shared that tidbit of information. If the car didn't pick up speed soon he'd find himself in the full force of the damn storm and the last thing he needed was more time away from the office.

The only reason he'd gone into the city had been to speak with his lawyer about acquiring two more parcels of land next to his shipbuilding business, and that hadn't been smooth sailing. The junk parcels of land, which had been vacant for a good thirty years, had out-of-town owners. Once they'd gotten a hint a person wanted them they'd sent down someone to investigate him, which he'd discovered thanks to his loyal work crew. While a part of him would like to beat the shit out of the guy who'd dug into his past, Paul knew that would accomplish nothing. So his jaunt into the city had been two-fold. Deal with his lawyer and hire his own private investigator. He wanted to know who was tipping off the locals that Paul Carter was looking to expand his business because his gut told him it was his rival from Newport and that wouldn't do. Millions of dollars were at stake and more importantly, hundreds of good paying jobs for his home town. That meant more to Paul than the money even though he tried hard never to let on.

Flicking the station in the hopes of finding a song more uplifting than the sappy love song requiem the stations seemed to like to play these days, it took all his driving instincts not to slam into the car in front of him spinning out of control like a spin the bottle. Thankful once again he'd gotten the studs put on his tires, he finally managed to gain control of the vehicle. Helplessly, he watched the red Mini Cooper take out an old mailbox only to come to a stop in the ditch.

Careful to pull off the road as much as possible, Paul jumped out of his truck and dashed to help the driver from the car.

Relying on instincts, he opened the driver side door and felt the punch to his gut. There out cold with a gash to her head was the last person he'd thought to ever see again. Ella O'Connor, his first steady girlfriend and the love of his life who had left him for greener pastures without as much as a goodbye. With his heart tripping in anxiety, Paul unclipped her seat belt, which thankfully had kept her from flying through the window and pulled her out. God, she weighed next to nothing in his arms. Hauling her into his truck, he quickly fished out his first aid kit. The gash wasn't that bad but what concerned him more was the bump swelling up like a goose's egg on her forehead. She mumbled and he thanked the heavens she was coming around.

She blinked up, and those hazel eyes of hers snagged him. Damn, if Paul didn't feel like a teenager again, all tongue-tied and embarrassed with how happy he was to see her.

"Ella. Ella...Ella come on now wake up. Keep those eyes open, honey, I'm taking you in to see the doctor."

She blinked again and finally focused on him. "Paul, is that you?"

He smiled. "Yeah, it is."

"The car, what happened?"

"Your car slipped on the icy road. I'll get one of my guys to haul it out for you. I'm going to buckle you up and I'm taking you into the walk-in clinic up the road. The snow's coming down heavy and there's no way we'll make it to the city for the hospital." While he talked he propped her up and buckled her in, noticing she'd cut her copper hair short, giving her a pixie look he liked. Too groggy to do much of anything, she let him manhandle her and that worried Paul. Ella had always been feisty and he prayed she wasn't more seriously hurt.

Turning on the truck, he cranked up the heat and opened his cell. He punched in a number he knew by heart. Calling in a favor would be worth it.

"Rob, its Paul. Yeah, listen. I've got Ella O'Connor in my truck. She was just in a car accident and ...Jesus Rob, I know that but we're in the thick of a Nor'easter and we can't turn around for the big hospital. I don't think she's seriously hurt, more bumped her head and all but will you...Thanks man. See you in less than ten at the clinic."

Paul talked to Ella the entire time, not sure she heard him but she mumbled the occasional answer. Sweat trickled down Paul's back from the damn heat in the truck but he knew Ella was probably in shock and needed the heat so he suffered in silence. When he finally pulled up at the clinic, Rob stood in the door with a nurse on hand.

Paul pulled up in front and jumped out to gently remove Ella from his truck. He carried her inside and placed her in the waiting wheelchair, backing away to let Dr. Robert Craig, the guy he'd saved from a sailing accident two years ago and who was also the best doctor Riverton had within miles, work his magic.

Wiping his sweaty palms on his dress pants, Paul didn't dare interrupt Rob. Only once he was finished did he step forward. "Will she be okay?"

"I think so. That's a nasty bump but I think it's more superficial. I think she's more in shock than anything else but I'm going to keep her under observation for a few hours. I guess she heard her mother had a stroke."

"What?"

"It was minor one, but Tara brought her in yesterday and she was released a few hours ago in fact," said Rob.

"Is that normal? Shouldn't you have kept her for observation?"

Rob gave him a look Paul didn't like. "Listen Paul, there's not much you can do for a minor stroke except let the patient heal. We'll keep an eye on Ella for a couple hours and if there's any change I'll let you know, okay?"

"Yeah, that'd be great. Thanks again Rob. I didn't know who else to call."

Rob grinned. "Good thing I was already on duty. Ella's going to have to take it slow for the next few days but I'm sure she'll be okay."

"Thanks," said Paul, not wanting to leave.

"Not much you can do here, Paul. Why don't you touch base with Tara and for Christ sakes when you call don't scare that girl. She's had a rough couple days already. Tell her to call me and I'll fill her in on her sister, okay?"

"She's got your number?" asked Paul, filing that tidbit of information away for closer examination later.

"Don't even go there, Paul. She's got my number because of her mother and nothing more. Listen, I've got to go and attend to our latest patient," said Rob, leaving Paul to do as instructed.

Paul didn't really want to leave the hospital but Rob was right. There wasn't much more he could do for Ella except touch base with her family. First though, he'd get one of his guys to haul Ella's car out of the ditch and tow it to the garage for her. Taking a deep breath, he realized he was still holding Ella's scarf. Scrunching up the warm wool in his hands, he waited until he was back in his truck to take a sniff and damn if Ella's scent didn't slam into him like her car almost had. That light flowery scent of lilac had been her signature perfume all through her high school years and it excited Paul to know some things about Ella hadn't changed.

Chapter Three

"Seriously, Mom. I'm fine. You're the one who's supposed to take it easy."

"Looks to me you're the one worse for wear," said her mother, giving her another cup of tea only to turn back to her task at hand—finishing up six pies. Not one pie. Six. Yup, not much had changed with her mother. And worry for her mother, who stood at the kitchen counter rolling out perfectly rounded pie shells, knotted through Ella. She hadn't realized how much she'd missed being home but everything, including how the house smelled like a mixture of desserts and fresh linen felt comfortable, inviting and warm. The thought of her house going to ruin much like Mary Beckman's had made her uncomfortable. Their house was a family home and had been passed down through the O'Connor generations for close to one hundred years. It certainly wasn't perfect and would never grace the pages of the magazines like the homes in Newport, but none of that truly mattered to Ella. It was the house of her childhood, with the crooked wooden stairs and the house of her angry teen years, where she'd gotten into the habit of slamming her bedroom door so much that the handle had fallen off. The thought of it, the house and the memories, turning to dust someday left her feeling slightly queasy.

"Isn't she supposed to be taking it easy?" asked Ella to her sister Tara, who walked into the kitchen and promptly rolled her eyes like she'd heard it all before. They both had, but things had changed. And change wasn't always good.

Tara had turned into a young woman and Ella made a mental note to spend more time with her younger sister. While Tara had embraced technology and religiously Skyped once a week with Ella, thanks to Ella giving her younger sister a computer and phone for Christmas about three years ago, nothing bridged the gap of years past like seeing her sister and mother in the flesh. Ella realized she'd missed Tara's high school prom, which had been around the same time she'd graduated with her law degree. It was a memory she could never recapture but she mentally made a vow to get more involved with her family.

"Seriously, Mom, six pies. I'm sure the ladies at the auxiliary will understand if you show up with one. You're not supposed to go overboard. You've only been home less than a day and I don't know about you but I've had enough of hospitals for a while," said Tara, taking Ella's cup of tea for herself. Tara knew Ella hated tea but good O'Connor daughters were supposed to be tea drinkers.

"What's the difference between one and six? It's nothing. You girls stop worrying. I'm just going to do up these pies and oh..."

"Oh what, Mom?" asked Ella, getting up to rifle through the kitchen cupboards for some coffee. At 10 am Ella would take any coffee, except decaf. She'd even take a cup of instant and what do you know, that's exactly what she found buried way in the back of her mother's baking cupboard.

Tara placed the kettle on the stove while Ella tried to dig out chunks of what had to be the oldest instant coffee ever into a mug. *Beggars can't be choosers.* Silently Ella prayed that the caffeine in the dried up instant coffee was still active. After spending hours in the hospital yesterday she felt both foolish and bruised. She knew when she'd touched base with Tara yesterday that her poor sister didn't need to be worrying about her while dealing with their mother, and while partly relieved Tara had laughed at her foolish accident she'd also expressed amazement when Ella had told her who her knight in shining armor was. Tara in her usual manner had spouted to her that it was destiny, but Ella wasn't so sure about that. Destiny had nothing to do with it, more like stupidity for her picking out a Mini to hit the winter roads of Newport.

Ella kept watching her mother. She noticed that while active, she was slower. Her mother was careful with how she laid out the pies and Ella couldn't help but notice how her hands trembled more.

"Well, I don't feel up to driving so I'm wondering if one of you gals will take me into town so I can drop off the pies."

Ella turned and glared at her mother. "Mom. I'll drop off the pies and you are having a nap this afternoon. I'll make sure to tell the ladies you made all six pies, but that it. You are not coming with me and you really are having a nap." To emphasize her point, Ella placed her hands on her hips.

"Why Ella I think that's a great idea. Thanks so much for offering to do this for me."

Ella's mother, Gwen O'Connor who by this point had flour all over her worn apron, smiled sweetly at Ella and like that Ella knew she'd been outfoxed. Her mother never had any intention of going into town and just like old times Ella had fallen for it.

Looking at Tara who hadn't said one word and who was quietly buttering toast, Ella was about to offer to suggest that her sister's help but then realized getting out would be good for her. Certainly better than staying home feeling like the worst heel possible for crashing her rental car. Plus last night she'd realization she'd lost her cellphone in the process. On top of that, her savior of the day had turned out to be none other than Paul Carter—her high school sweetheart and the boy who had turned into one handsome man she'd never gotten over. Ella definitely needed to escape her memories. She could have sworn yesterday he'd called her honey, but she wondered if her mild concussion was playing tricks on her.

Just thinking about yesterday made her head ache. Pouring water into her mug and giving the dried chunks of instant coffee a hard stir, Ella replied to her mother, "Not a problem."

"And dear, when you go into town do stop in and give this bag of cookies to Paul will you?" said her mother, who was now layering all six pies with sliced apples.

"What?"

"Paul said to give you these when he stopped by this morning," said her mother, whipping out her rental car keys from her pant pockets. "He said your car's been towed to the garage and thought you might need the keys for the rental agency. Oh, and he said you shouldn't drive that car anymore. What were you thinking getting a Mini when you know what our weather is like here?"

Calmly Ella sipped at her black coffee and winced. It wasn't the heat that hurt her taste buds, rather the strong force of the brew. "Paul was here?"

"That's what I just said. You were in the shower so I promised him I'd give them to you."

"Mom please tell me you didn't tell him I was in the shower," said Ella, feeling her face heat because that's exactly what her mother admitted to like it was no big deal.

"Mom, seriously, next time a guy comes to the house just tell him we're busy."

Placing two pies on the top burner and two on the bottom, Gwen turned to look at her girls. "Well, Tara since we don't get many guys coming to our house I guess I'm out of practice."

This time those piercing blue eyes of Gwen's looked steadily at both her daughters.

"Well, most mothers would be pleased with that."

"No they wouldn't. You, Tara need to date and you Ella...well...oh, I don't know."

But Ella did. Her mother wanted grandchildren and she'd made that plain as natural butter with no subtlety at all. Every conversation Ella had with her mother centered not on work but rather if she'd met someone. Ella had met someone but she still hadn't confessed that to her family. And why was that? It was a question that haunted her. As great a guy as Craig Kinley was, why was it so hard for Ella to confess she'd not only met someone six months ago but had recently become engaged. It was a good thing Craig was away on business or else he'd have wanted to accompany Ella to her hometown and Ella certainly wasn't ready for that.

"Everything okay, Ella? You're looking a little pale yourself," said her mom.

"I'm fine, but I just remembered I've lost my cell and I've got to call into work to check on a few things."

"Well, dear seems to me any old phone will do, even one that's still attached to a wall."

Ella looked at her mother and smiled. "Guess you're right. It's just that all my contacts were on that phone. Serves me right. I should have backed them up on a cloud."

"Now, dear I have no idea what you're talking about...but a cloud? Seriously, where do they come up with these sayings?" said Gwen, causing Ella and Tara to both burst into giggles.

Ella and Tara exchanged a look. "Okay, Mom we're not ganging up on you. I'll drop in to thank Paul and drop off your pies. Do you need me to pick up anything else in town?"

Promptly her mother smiled at them both and turned to pick up a nearby piece of paper to write down a very detailed grocery list for Ella, who fought not to groan. She wasn't sure if it was the thought of getting the groceries or seeing Paul again that made her stomach dip with nervousness but she vowed she'd be adding two other necessary things to her mother's list—a coffee maker and coffee beans. There was no way Ella was going to survive two more weeks without her coffee, especially when it felt like her mother was back in true fighting form and picking on her.

Later that afternoon after the pies had cooled to her mother's satisfaction, Ella found herself being hugged by more women than at a funeral parlor. With a tight smile lining her face she answered their pointed questions about her mother, her and even her sister. All of her mother's friends, who promptly arranged for each and every one of them to bring over supper for her dear oh-so-not ailing mother, were horrified to learn that Gwen had been in the hospital. Guess that's why her mother had been avoiding answering the phone all day. She hadn't wanted to tell them and what better messenger than Ella. After slowly extracting herself from her mother's friends, Ella spent a good hour in the grocery store. Sitting inside the warm truck, she knew she was stalling. She didn't want to go thank Paul. In fact she wanted to never see him again. Not because she hated him - after all she was the one who had ended things. No, because the heartache of what they had was something she'd never been able to forget. But Ella O'Connor wasn't a coward and her mother had instilled manners in all her daughters, so Ella started up the truck and slowly pulled out of the lot to hit the main drag. Reporting that she'd failed to thank her savior of the day would only earn her a stern lecture from her mother and make her feel worse.

About thirty minutes later she pulled onto another secondary road and almost drove past what had been the Carter shipyard. The driveway she pulled into didn't look a thing like how her childhood memories remembered. Back then she'd crawled over enough decaying fishing vessels to know the place had been quite literally rotting away and Danny Carter, Paul's father hadn't cared one whit. He'd spent most of his time drinking away whatever earnings he'd made from fixing the boats. Obviously all that had changed. *Just when,* Ella wondered as she pulled her mother's truck into a neat perfectly paved parking lot.

A white two storey building was to the left and neatly stacked rows of twenty-foot yachts sat to the right, perched on wooden rungs while workers fixed them. Scanning the place quickly, she counted a good forty people coming and going and smiled. Paul certainly had made good on his childhood promise. He'd always wanted to make it big in their small town and when she'd told him staying in Riverton wouldn't make that dream come true, guess she was wrong for once.

"So what do you think, Ella?" said Paul

Sweet Jesus, she hadn't seen him come out of the office and just like old times she was reminded how he liked to sneak up on her to scare the wits out of her.

"I think I owe you a big thank you and this place looks amazing. Mom insisted I drop these off to you. I bet they're your favorite double-chocolate chip cookies."

He smiled and that dimple on his right cheek she so used to love kissing flashed at her. Her stomach dipped with longing and she felt her face heat. Damn, she was acting like a teenager around him. Pulling herself together, Ella returned his smile.

He took the paper bag from her and their fingers gently touched. It was an innocent touch but the affect was instant. Ella felt all those butterflies she tried hard to ignore flutter like a thousand wings, caressing her entire body with a longing she had no right to.

"Thanks so much. These cookies won't last five seconds in the office. Your mom's cookies are the best and the guys in the office tend to smell them the minute I'm lucky enough to get my hands on some. I'm so glad it was me tailing you yesterday. It's not often I get to play superhero."

"Well you played it well. I don't remember much after the crash but I gathered from the clinic staff you drove me in yourself. Thanks again Paul."

"It's the least I could do. Are you sure you're totally okay? And how's your mom, Ella? I only had the chance to speak with her for a bit this morning when I dropped off your keys, and that reminds me, please tell me you're not getting another Mini from that rental agency."

His eyes narrowed like they used to when he was intently watching her, trying to figure out if she was telling the whole truth. Funny how she missed that look of his. Ella chuckled, softly. "Nope. I'm done with small. I'll just use Mom's pickup truck while I'm here. Plus I don't think they'd rent to me again after they see the car. Mom's doing okay but you know how she is."

"Stubborn, determined to do it her own way and not wanting anyone to worry about her. A trait I think both you and your sister inherited if I recall, or have things changed since you moved to the big city?"

There it was. The city jibe she'd heard about four times already today. First from her mother's friendly friends with their city innuendos and then she'd had the not-so-good luck of snagging a cashier at the grocery store from high school who'd made enough city puns to leave Ella feeling uncomfortable.

"Nope. I'm still the same," said Ella.

"Ella I didn't mean anything by that remark. Seeing you in that car crash threw me yesterday. Not sure I'll ever recover from that. Listen, I had one of my guys tow your car to Frank's garage and he said considering how you landed the car's not that bad."

Ella watched Paul run his hands through his hair. In the years since she'd last seen him, he'd filled out. Somewhere over the course of a decade he'd turned from boy to man. And while Ella tried hard to make like she wasn't checking him out she suspected she was failing. Maybe he joined a gym. Paul had always been good looking but he hadn't had the football player physique and all that had changed. His dark, wavy brown hair was cut shorter but everything else had changed. Instead of wearing jeans like most everyone else in the yard he was wearing sharp dress pants and hadn't bothered to throw on a winter jacket. His dress shirt was a deep blue, bringing out the sky-blue color of his eyes. He looked so different from what she thought he'd look like that she felt a little overwhelmed and certainly underdressed. She was wearing a pair of worn jeans, practical boots and a short bomber jacket. Not her normal New York attire but certainly comfortable and respectable enough for home, or so she'd thought.

A Jeep pulled into the side parking lot, narrowly missing a parked car. Paul's look turned stoic. "Listen, I've got to go, but I'm really glad you're okay. No more Minis. Tell your mom I'll pop by tomorrow for that pie she promised me and tell her thanks for the cookies."

Ella wanted to say something but Paul took off across the lot too fast for her to formulate a polite response. And what the heck was her mother doing making pies for Paul? With formalities over with, Ella went to get back into her mother's truck, trying hard not to pay attention to Paul speaking with the frantic woman who had pulled into his lot.

The woman, who was obviously mad as hell didn't seem to care that she was causing a scene at Paul's workplace. Dressed in fashionable black high heeled boots with a matching black mini skirt, which meant hopefully she was freezing her ass off, she was drop dead gorgeous.

"Why he lets that woman do that to him pisses me off," said a man to another worker walking past Ella.

"He'll get Debbie settled down in five minutes. You watch," said the second guy.

Then it hit Ella. That was Paul's Debbie, who he married five years ago. That queasy feeling she'd had earlier returned two-fold. Getting into the truck, Ella started the engine and slowly backed up. She noticed Paul haul Debbie into his office and more than anything Ella knew she had to make sure she wasn't around tomorrow when he dropped in for her mother's pie. Seeing Paul again awoke those old loving memories, ones she'd thought long buried. She might be a lawyer now and didn't like to think of herself as a coward but seeing Paul with another woman wasn't something she could handle. She wasn't saying the coward word, just more like chicken.

Chapter Four

Paul was furious. Seeing Debbie usually did that to him and the timing couldn't be worse. He'd been so excited to see Ella pull up in her mother's pick-up truck that he'd dashed out of his office without grabbing his suit jacket. She'd looked bruised and still a little shaken but otherwise she was still as beautiful as ever. He'd wanted to ask her how long she would be staying but hadn't mustered his courage. Now, as he sat listening to his ex-wife's tirade he wished once again she'd never entered his life. The divorce had been sort of settled a little over a year ago but in truth their marriage had been a sham from the get-go. Two years ago he'd been the one to move out after Debbie had done her best to make his life a living hell. Not more than six weeks went by without her talking with her lawyer asking for more of his hard-earned dough.

Today, he once again cursed himself for having allowed Debbie to sweep him off his feet with her pretend charm and even frostier heart. The only reason he even agreed to marry her was she pulled out the 'I'm pregnant card' and instant guilt had slammed into him. Two months into his marriage she said she'd miscarriage but Paul often wondered if she'd been pregnant in the first place. From day one the marriage had been stormy and Paul had suffered four years with her, spending more and more time at the office or the bar, enough to dread going home. The only out would be for him to pack his bags, which he'd done two years ago. Debbie didn't like being dumped, not that she let on to anyone he'd been the one to end their marriage. Honestly, he didn't care. Life was better when she was miles away.

"Debbie, seriously why are you here?" That had to be the fifth time he'd asked her but as usual she was attempting to wind him up for some long drawn saga of an affair.

"I'm pregnant," she said.

Paul didn't say a thing. All he thought was thank god it wasn't his. "And?"

"And…is that all you've got to say to me, after all we've been through."

"Darlin' we've been over for years in case you haven't noticed but you didn't come here to drop this on me. What's the real reason?" He kept his voice calm and measured when he really want to kick the bitch out the door. Paul might not have been raised great thanks to his deadbeat, drinking dad but Mrs. O'Connor had always shown him manners meant something and he'd always liked her attitude. Plus he'd always liked her daughter—Ella. Lost in his thought of the first time he'd seen Ella in kindergarten class, he picked up a file folder and moved it away from Debbie's prying eyes. The last thing he wanted her to know were the plans he was attempting to set in motion to secure the other two lots. Property that would certainly help line his pockets but if she had an inkling of his plans she'd make him pay big time.

"Paul, I don't want this kid. I'd make a terrible mother."

Paul wasn't so certain of that but it wasn't his problem. "Listen, this isn't my problem but if you're looking for some cash to get away to think about this I'll give you some."

She smiled, and it instantly softened her looks. "I'd need about three thousand."

Paul stood up from the chair he'd been sitting in. "Get real, Debbie. I'm not handing you over three thousand. I'll give you half that and expect you not to come back bothering me. And, you might want to inform the lucky guy about his impending fatherhood."

"Maybe," she answered.

Paul went to his safe and quickly counted out the bills. Debbie took them without saying a word. That is until she got to the door. "Who was that woman I saw you talking with?"

"What?"

"That woman who got in the old pick-up truck, who was she?"

"No one. Just a woman looking for a quote on a small boat. I told her we don't have time for small jobs. Why?"

"Oh, nothing. Heard a rumor in town your old girlfriend was home for the holiday."

Paul shrugged and carefully kept his face impassive. The last thing he wanted was Debbie to ever meet Ella. Debbie's claws could be lethal and Ella wouldn't stand a chance. "She usually stays with her mom when she visits."

"Seems to me the last time she was here we were engaged."

Paul sat back down in his chair. "Debbie, I've got a lot of work ahead of me here. Now that you're settled and you've got what you came for, I really don't have time to chat."

"We could go in to that back room of yours just like old time's sake," she said, flashing him a sexy smile.

His stomach churned. God, at one time they'd practically had sex in every corner of the boatyard. He'd been a lucky bastard to escape her clutches. Paul looked up and sliced her a look. "Why don't you do something right Debbie and call the father to be."

This time she stormed out the door and Paul welcomed the sound of the door slamming hard behind her. He silently prayed the money he'd handed over to her would keep her away while Ella was in town.

The next morning, after spending a restless night thinking about Ella, he mustered his courage and drove over to her mother's house. About ten inches of snow had fallen overnight but still her driveway was cleared. Paul bet that was Ella's doing. She'd always liked getting up early and as much as he tried to be chivalrous and had offered to shovel her mother's long driveway after their father had died, she'd politely but firmly refused. She might have spouted that she liked the exercise but he suspected it had more to do with pride than anything else.

Parking his truck at the side of the house, he got out and started to the back where Ella was sitting on a snow bank, obviously winded from her shoveling workout.

"Want some help?"

She squealed and sank further into the fluffy snowbank. "Why do you keep scaring me?"

Paul walked over and held out his hand to haul Ella up from her homemade seat of snow. "That wasn't my intention. I didn't even know you were there. Thought for sure you'd be inside warming up."

Ella pulled the tight wool cap down a little lower on her exposed ears and Paul couldn't help but notice how red her earlobes looked. She dusted off the snow pants she was wearing and adjusted her scarf. And that reminded Paul he hadn't returned her scarf from the accident.

"Warming up will have to wait. I've got to shovel the path to the barn for Tara."

Paul took the shovel from her. "I'll do that. You go in and warm up. You look almost frozen," he said, taking another step toward her.

She attempted to grab the shovel out of his hand and he quickly shuffled it behind his back. They'd done this same shovel dance a few times during their high school days and he couldn't help but smile. Ella laughed and the sound travelled straight to his heart.

"Seriously, Paul I can shovel."

"And so can I. Listen though, I'd love a cup of coffee and your mom promised me a pie. Give me twenty minutes and I'll be inside. But," he moved closer so that their warm puffy jackets were almost touching. "Please tell your mom no tea and please tell me you brought some coffee with you because honestly, as much as I'd hate to be impolite to your mother I can't stomach that instant stuff she keeps."

Ella laughed so hard she had to clutch her stomach, making Paul laugh. He wasn't sure what was so funny but he damn well wanted to know so he could get her hazel eyes to light up like the color of fresh spring grass again.

"I hear you. I had to buy a coffee press and ground beans yesterday when I was picking up groceries. I almost died that first day when I had to use the instant coffee I found buried in her baking cupboard."

"Oh my god, you didn't," he said, realizing his heart was beating extra hard. *We're flirting.* The realization made his smile a little broader. Paul wasn't expecting miracles but he'd take the stolen moments he could get with Ella, the one girl who he'd let walk out of his life and the only one to capture his heart completely.

"Oh yeah, I did. It was horrible. The first thing I did when I got into town was hit that new coffee house."

"You mean Ground Beans," answered Paul.

"Yeah, that was it. I remember a few years ago that place had been a rundown shack. They did a really great job with the renovations."

"And the best part is that because they did it others are following. I heard there's plans for a nice restaurant going in two doors down."

"Really? Wow, something other than a pizzeria, please."

"I'd agree with you. We've got about ten of those. One of the guys who works for me said his brother was planning a nice Greek family restaurant."

"How many guys do you employ?"

"This time of year I've got sixty full-time and once spring hits that will double. So have we got a deal, Ella O'Connor?"

"Deal?"

"Yeah, my shoveling services for coffee and pie."

"Oh yeah, we've got a deal. I know when I've been outmaneuvered. Plus my ears are killing me."

Paul couldn't help himself. He took a step forward and using his hand pulled her wool cap even lower over her ears. It brought her up and close to him and the smell of her strawberry shampoo hit him. "There. Now, get in that house and warm up. I'll see you soon. I like my coffee black in case you're wondering."

"If I recall you used to like it with three sugars."

This time Paul chuckled. "Some things had to change. At my age I don't need those calories," he said, moving down the path with the shovel to begin clearing a second lane from the house to the barn. Paul could have sworn he heard Ella mumbling something under her breath but he couldn't make it out. With a smile firmly planted on his lips he started his task. The sweet reward of having pie and coffee with Ella was firmly planted in his mind and the sooner he got finished shoveling that tempting morsel was his.

Chapter Five

The water was about to boil but it took about another minute for Ella to get it off the stove. She was glued to the window. Watching Paul shovel snow shouldn't be that fascinating but even the whine of the kettle wasn't getting her attention like Paul's backside. Five minutes into it, he'd shed his thick blue winter jacket to rest on the frame of his SUV. He wore a fisherman's knitted sweater and dark blue jeans. And every time he bent over, Ella had a mighty fine view of his ass. Intense longing hit her and she found herself kicking herself. She should have toughed it out and finished the path to the barn. What the heck was she doing staring at Paul Carter like some love sick teenager? He was off limits. Too bad her heart and body liked it so much they were ignoring her rational, logical mind that said step away from temptation.

"Oh, I'm so glad he stopped by," said her mother.

"Stopped by? Yesterday you made him cookies and today you promised him a thank you pie. What did you expect?"

"My, someone got up on the wrong side of bed this morning."

Okay Ella deserved that. She was snapping at her mother when she was really mad at herself. "Sorry, Mom. It's just that..."

Cursing at herself, she was not going to admit her feelings for Paul had not been buried deep like the snow outside.

Her mother came closer to her and eyed what Ella had been watching. "Deep down, Paul's the same boy you knew but I'd say he turned into one fine looking man."

The high pitched whistle from the kettle save Ella from commenting. Tearing her eyes away from Paul was hard but confessing to her mother how much she'd longed for Paul over the years was not up for discussion.

In the kitchen, she slowly poured the water from the kettle into the new Bodum she'd purchased.

"Not like you to walk away from a challenge, Ella."

Ella stifled a groan. "He's not the same, Mom. For one he's married."

"No he's not," said Gwen calmly letting her knife slide into the now cooled pecan pie she'd obviously made for Paul. It had been his favorite pie since elementary days and Ella was fairly certain that hadn't changed.

With a calm she didn't feel, Ella took out two mugs. "What do you mean?"

"Oh, Ella I thought for sure your sister would have told you. He and Debbie split a couple years ago and I know from one of the ladies at the auxiliary that his divorce was finalized a year ago. You know, he moved out. Good thing too. She was a gold digger. Never really cared for him one whit if you asked me."

Ella did things on automatic. She poured the coffee into the mugs, and set the table in the kitchen. When the back door opened she heard some stamping and knew Paul was getting the snow off his boots. She also knew he'd remove his boots and in a minute would be in her mother's kitchen just like old times. Inside though Ella was reeling. *He's not married. He got a divorce. Why had no one told me? Because I hadn't asked.*

With her heart racing, Ella turned to her mother. "Sorry, I totally forgot I've got to make this important phone call to the office. It's going to take a while. Tell Paul thank you for me, but I've really got to go," said Ella, racing out of her mother's kitchen leaving Gwen with a bewildered look on her face.

Ella darted to her room, locked the door and tried to calm down. Paul was downstairs in her kitchen now chatting politely with her mother, eating his pie and drinking her coffee. Damn, in Ella's haste to escape she'd forgotten her coffee.

Not sure what to do, Ella got interrupted from her train-wreck of thoughts by a soft knock on her bedroom door. She knew that knock and hoped her mother wasn't in the mood to give her a lecture. Opening the door, Ella also flicked open her cell she's retrieved yesterday from the rental car. Pretending like she was talking to someone in the office was her lifeline at the moment.

Without a word, her mother walked in and set down her coffee. Only at the door did Gwen turn and say, "Paul's gone, Ella. Said he had lots of work to do and was sorry you couldn't spare him five minutes."

"He said that?" Ella said, forgetting she was supposed to be pretending to listen to her make believe person on the other end of her cell.

Her mother gave her a pointed look, which instantly made Ella feel bad. "No he didn't say that. He's too polite. What's gotten into you? I hope all that time living in the big city hasn't erased all my lessons on being polite."

Ella fought not to cry. She was thirty years old and honestly didn't need this but her mother was right. Giving up the pretense, she closed her phone. "I...I..."

Gwen sat down on Ella's bed and patted the spot next to her. "Paul has never forgotten you Ella. He asks about you every Christmas."

Oh god do I really want to hear this? I guess I do. Sitting beside her mother, she settled in for a long mother-daughter talk.

"Mom, it's not as easy as picking up where we left off. You're forgetting I dumped him."

"I think he knew you needed time away."

"Seriously, Mom, I've been away for years now. What we had was a high school crush on each other. He got married."

"And divorced."

"Yes, he got divorced, but I'm sure Paul isn't interested in me. I've changed." *I'm engaged but don't have the guts to tell you.*

"And so has he. Both of you are older and hopefully smarter. All I'm saying is go with your heart. Paul's a nice guy. He's done a lot for this community. That young man took his father's shipbuilding business and turned it into one of the most lucrative businesses on this shore."

"That's great," said Ella, meaning it, but her mother wasn't listening to her. "Mom, I'm not staying. I can't stay. In another week I'll be back in

New York so it's not like anything can happen." *I've got a great life there.* Why did that sound lame?

"Why can't you stay?"

This time Ella sighed. She'd had this conversation a few times already since she'd arrived and more recently with herself. "Mom, I'm a real estate lawyer."

"And, are you saying we don't have real estate to sell here? Seems to me this town is changing. Might be a good time to get in on the ground floor and make a name for yourself here. You do know there's at least five buildings up for sale on Main Street, and two of the ladies in my auxiliary are planning to sell and trust me those homes, in the right hands would sell for a fortune."

"Mom, I don't sell real estate. I do up the contracts for the land and buildings."

"Well, what if you had a partner?"

Ella fought not to groan. How come she'd let this conversation get so off course? *Oh, I know, because I don't want to talk about my feelings for Paul and haven't even mentioned Craig to my family.* Not talking about it felt safer than opening a can of worms. "Mom, the thing is I don't have a partner, and I've got a good paying job in New York."

Her mother got up from her bed and hugged her. "I'm sorry hon. I know you have a great job and I'm so proud of you. I've just missed you so much, Ella and so has your sister. It's nice you're home for the holidays. I won't bug you again. I'm just letting you know you could make it here. Paul certainly has and who would have thought that?"

Well if that wasn't a jab at her nothing was. Her mother was throwing down the gauntlet. With those parting words her mother made her exit. Ella picked up her now cold coffee and took a sip thinking on her mother's words. Could she make it here? Paul had but he was in a field that this community was known for. Still though, she had seen a number of for sale signs up around town, including a sorry looking for sale sign on Mrs. Beckman's farm house.

Just for fun, Ella pulled out her laptop and searched up homes for sale in the area. Two hours later another knock sounded on her door.

"Sorry, thought you said you wouldn't be doing work while you were here?" asked her sister, looking annoyed.

Ella jumped up off the bed and grabbed a sweater. She had been so engrossed in her research she hadn't realized how cold the old house had gotten but the large goose bumps on her arms couldn't be ignored. Rubbing her arms, she said, "I wasn't doing work. Just checking on a few things mom said."

"Yeah, mom told me you just found out about Paul and Debbie. Listen, about that, I'm sorry. I thought since you never asked about Paul you either knew or didn't want to know," said Tara, chewing on her bottom lip.

Ella pulled her sister in for a hug. "No worries. I should have asked. It's just that the thought of him being married hurt so I honestly didn't want to talk about him."

Tara pulled back. "You do know that Debbie's a bitch, right?"

Ella laughed. "Well, I might have thought of her like that without even meeting her but I'm sure she's an alright person."

Tara shook her head. "She's not. She played Paul from the get go."

"I'm sure they had feelings for each other, but enough. I don't want to talk about Paul. I'm going to go into town for a bit this afternoon. You want to come?"

Tara looked out Ella's bedroom window. "I can't. But can you drop off some of my work to a few clients?"

Ella smiled. "I would love to. And Tara girl you promised to show me some of your new stuff. I'm not leaving until you show me what you're working on for hours at a time in that barn."

Tara's cheeks turned red. "It's just some stuff."

"Okay, I won't pry. But, I'm really proud of what you're doing. I don't have a creative bone in my body so I'm thrilled you got all those genes. Did mom ever show you some of the paintings Dad did?" asked Ella.

"Yeah, she did."

"He had talent, but he took the safe route. He'd be real proud of what you're doing with your life, Tara."

"Safe sounds good when you're not sure when the next piece will sell and you've got bills to pay."

Ella gave her sister a thorough look. "Didn't you mention that there was a secret buyer who's been gobbling up your stuff?"

Tara blushed. "Yeah, it's been wonderful."

"He's buying your stuff because it's great. What you create with your pottery is one of a kind. Listen, we'll talk more when I get back. If I don't head into town the places will close up."

"What are you doing in town?"

"Don't tell Mom, but I'm following up on something she said."

"And," fished her sister.

This time it was Ella looking awkward. "I really don't want to say anything until I know more."

"Okay, enough. I'm going to bundle up my stuff. It'll take me a good hour."

"Good, that gives me time to grab a hot shower and another cup of hot coffee," said Ella, walking down the hall to the washroom as her sister sprinted down the stairs.

Ella turned on the shower and waited for the ancient hot water heater to kick in before she dared step inside. The more she thought about what she'd been researching the more she smiled. One thing was for certain, Ella knew she'd have to make sure her mother didn't get wind of what she was looking into. Until Ella researched the idea to death she was keeping her mouth shut. The last thing she wanted was any gossip reaching her mother and that meant she'd have to be very careful while she poked around.

Chapter Six

Paul was fuming mad. More at himself, acting like a fool for Ella all over again. He should have known better. Nothing good was going to come of wishing for what he couldn't have, which was Ella in his life and most certainly in his bed. Too bad all his memories of Ella had surfaced, leaving him all but panting with need. She's been his first girl. When they'd kissed that first time their teeth had clashed and they'd laughed and then gotten it right the second, third and fourth times.

His fist slammed into the weight bag with enough force to almost make him curse out loud. Damn if that didn't hurt. The used boxing gloves had taken the brunt of the sting off his hands but he wanted pain. He did his usual repeat pounding session on the punching bag for another fifteen minutes, feeling the burn in his lungs and hands. He was glad now he'd insisted on hanging the weight from the reinforced wooden beam in the converted warehouse. The warehouse that at one time he'd thought of tearing down to make way for more boats. He was glad now he'd kept the building and had it fixed up for him and the crew.

Four years ago when he'd been going through hell and wanted to spend as little time as possible at his house he'd used his energies to convert the warehouse into a make-shift gym. When his crew found out what he was doing they'd slowly over the months added more stuff and today there were three treadmills, two heavy bags, about a dozen weights and even an elliptical. Christ, he'd kill to see one of his guys sweating on that elliptical. The only thing Paul had brought to the place had been the heavy bags but that didn't mean he didn't hit the treadmill for a good hour-long run when he needed to vent off steam.

"What's with the note?"

Paul cursed long and hard in his head. *Shit*. He didn't want Ella to be here to see him like this—angry. He kept up his rhythm. Sweat rolled down his back and he had to blink the sweat out of his eyes.

32

Ella came right up beside him and even through the stench of his own sweat he caught a whiff of her lilac perfume.

"What's with the note, Paul?'

Paul hit the bag hard. "I was just returning your scarf. Nothing to it."

"You're mad at me. Why?"

"Jesus, Ella, I was just trying to be nice and stay out of your way. You made it perfectly clear you didn't want me around today—"

"Oh, Paul, I'm sorry for being so rude. It's just that seeing you again...

Paul stopped punching and grabbed the nearby towel to wipe off. He waited for Ella to finish, knowing she wouldn't and hoping she would. He watched her struggle. She kept darting her eyes at his chest and he had to fight a grin. He knew he didn't look the same since they'd parted. A decade changed a man and he'd purposely bulked up. Gone was that scrawny, no-confidence kid looking for some loving from the one girl he thought would be his forever. Changing was easy but trying to forget Ella when he'd loved her with everything he had, had been harder. And now here she was, back in his life and that old familiar ache for her burned through his body and heart.

Not as academically smart as Ella, Paul had to learn things the old-fashioned way. He couldn't afford secondary education so he'd learned what needed to get done to make his business successful. That didn't mean every day for that first year when Ella had left he didn't wish for her to call to tell him she missed him as much as he missed her. The nights has been the hardest. For hours he'd lie in bed recalling her body, the things she'd said to him over the years and the feel of her soft kisses that always turned to passionate embraces when they could steal some time alone. As teenagers time alone hadn't been easy or all that comfortable but they hadn't cared.

Today, he was proud of what he'd accomplished. While his father hadn't given one whit about their community Paul did and he owed a lot of that to Ella and her mom. Ella was the one who wrapped her arms around the shy, awkward teen he'd been and whispered encouraging words when he talked about making changes to the shipyard. She had told him he could do it when no one else believe in him.

Back then though Paul had naively thought letting Ella go off to pursue her dream would ensure she'd come back to him. The last thing he'd wanted was to smother her but when she'd left, she hadn't looked back. Not one letter, not one email, not one visit home had she checked in on him. Damn, that hurt because Paul had always looked for her. The hardest times had been Christmas when he'd check in on Gwen with some flimsy excuse to see if she needed help with the wood or whatever. Paul always got the impression Ella's mother knew he was looking for her but all she'd say was Ella was busy studying or working in the big city. Paul had never been to New York and he had no intention of visiting any time soon because his dislike for the city that kept away his Ella from him and her family was real.

He walked by her to grab a drink from the nearby water cooler.

"This is hard for me, Paul. You've got to understand. I came home thinking you were still married."

"I'm not."

"Yeah, I finally figured that out, but ..."

"But what, Ella?"

"I don't want you to hate me."

Paul sighed and moved closer. "Ella, I could never hate you." He was so close he could smell her strawberry shampoo.

She took a step toward him. "I never expected this. When I crashed and you saved me I felt awkward and whenever I see you I get this..."

Jesus, if she paused one more time, Paul was going to do something drastic, like kiss those lips of hers. Just thinking about that caused his feet to move closer.

"Paul," she said.

Her voice was a whisper that felt more like an invitation and he was going to take it. Paul closed the gap, grasped her around the waist and hauled her close. He didn't give her time to react, he simply acted.

His lips descended and she met him halfway, open and willing. What might have been hesitant became desperate. They kissed like they had in high school, when they sneaked snuggles behind the bleachers or in her parent's barn, frantic for the feel of each other. Paul's hands snaked in underneath Ella's jacket, wanting the feel of her skin on his fingers. He changed his stance, angling his head more and her tongue met his. He groaned. She felt so good, so right, and so damned perfect in his arms he never wanted to let her go.

Her hands skimmed across his back, at first tentative but then with a desperate feel like she couldn't figure the best place to let them rest. Paul found himself moving her back toward the wall. The minute she hit the wood, he shucked off her jacket and moved his lips lower, kissing her neck. She groaned and ran one of her hands through his damp hair while the other skimmed over his back muscles.

Needing the taste of her again on his lips, Paul moved his lips back up to capture her eager mouth while cupping her face with one hand.

She angled her head and he skimmed light kisses down her neck and then lower as his hand cupped her breast. She groaned and clutched at him, pushing his head deeper into her, ensuring he understood her want. Paul almost chuckled. This was the Ella he knew and loved.

Her nipple pebbled thanks to his tentative mouth which was leaving a large wet stain on her shirt. Like she knew that, Ella whipped her shirt over her head.

Paul sank to his knees.

"What are you doing?" she asked with a breathless voice that caused his erection to strain even more against his gym pants.

Cupping her ass, he hauled her closer. His head was level with her cute belly button. "Worshipping you."

Her hands skimmed through his hair. "I like," she said.

"Trust me, I like more. God I've missed you, Ella."

"Paul..."

"Shh, less talk and more kissing."

She chuckled and he kissed her belly as it moved, causing her to giggle more. This was like old times. A lot of their foreplay had been spent learning each other's bodies and Ella happened to have a lot of ticklish places. Kissing the sides of her belly, he let his hands capture her plump breasts. With his fingers he tweaked her nipples, loving how sensitive they were to his touch. She was panting with need – something he understood. Edging up, his mouth captured her taut nipples and he suckled first one and then the other until she was squirming. His free hand tentatively moved lower to slip between the vee of her legs. More than anything he wanted to feel her heat but for now he'd take whatever she was willing to give him.

Ella opened her legs more and groaned. "God I want you Paul."

Those were the best five words Paul had ever heard. He was about to speak when she sank to his level. They were now both on their knees and kissing with all the heat and passion they'd been denied for years. When Ella's hand reached out to push against his erection Paul almost toppled over.

Her hand found his shape and within seconds thoughts of going slow vanished.

"You like?"

She was teasing him and he smiled around her lips. "Oh, yeah, I like."

"Paul, we can't..."

"Ella, are you in there?"

They both froze like two deer caught in headlights. With lightning fast reflexes Ella scampered to her feet and whipped on her shirt and jacket. Paul gritted his teeth and rearranged the part of him that was now left throbbing with need.

"You in there, Ella?"

"That's my sister," said Ella, her cheeks heating red with what Paul hoped was passion more than embarrassment. However, he highly suspected she felt like him—needy but trying to get it together. His heart was still beating a fast tempo and he cursed her sister's timing.

"I'm in here, Tara," said Ella, scouting around him before Tara got the wrong impression. For once she'd be correct with her assessment of the situation.

Tara stepped through the open door and took in the scene. Paul smiled at Ella and then walked over to the cooler to grab another drink of water. He needed to put more space between them because he ached to act like the fool and haul her over his shoulder and away to a much more private location so they could finish what they had started.

"Why are you here, Tara?" asked Ella, trying hard to zip up her boomer jacket. Paul was pleased to see her fumble. She was rattled and that's exactly how she made him feel.

Tara looked at both of them but Paul wasn't about to kiss and tell.

"I'm here because there's a guy at our house claiming to be your fiancé," said Tara, crossing her arms over her chest as she glared at her sister.

Paul waited a heartbeat for Ella to refute her sister's ridiculous claim. Instead Ella said, "Craig. Craig's at the house."

Tara moved closer to her sister. "Yes, Craig's at the house and Mom's playing hostess. Are you telling me what he's saying is true?"

Paul didn't wait to hear another word. He'd heard all he needed. Ella hadn't denied it. She was engaged.

"Guess congratulations are in order," said Paul, mustering his courage as he grabbed his shirt and strode past Ella and Tara. "Shut the door on your way out. It locks automatically."

He didn't look back. Ella certainly hadn't when she had left him and it was good to remember that. Better than recalling in vivid detail the taste of her lips or how wonderful she felt in his arms. Once again he was the one being played for a fool.

Chapter Seven

"I can't believe you didn't tell us," said Tara for the tenth time as they made their way up from Paul's workout building to the parking lot.

"Sorry," said Ella, again. She noticed immediately Paul's truck was gone. She wasn't sure if that was a blessing or not. She felt stupid, realizing she should have said something to Paul but what? *Yeah, Craig's my finance but I'm not sure how I really feel about him.* That sounded lame. She should know how she felt about Craig. It wasn't like he wasn't nice, good looking or prosperous but the hard reality was Craig didn't make her feel like Paul did.

Ella fought the tears that threatened to spill. Being wrapped in Paul's arms had made her recall how she felt whenever she was with him – a hot, wild woman. That had always been the way with Paul. Even when they were teenagers she'd been wild about the shy boy who turned out to be quite the opposite in the bedroom. Not that they had sampled each other once as teens in a bedroom – more like the barn, his father's hunting shack, and one especially vivid memory surfaced of them behind the bleachers at their high school football game.

"Well, it's a good thing I found you before you did something stupid with Paul."

Too late. Way too late. Ella kept quiet as they both unlocked their vehicles. She almost wished Paul had said something to her. But that wasn't his way. He wasn't like his father who would explode in anger. Paul, from an early age, always made an effort to channel his anger in another direction. Even when they were teens and she got angry at the injustice of her life that took away her father, who died suddenly of a massive heart attack, Paul would only offer the comfort of his arms and calming voice. *God I miss that.*

"Mom's really excited just so you know, but she's going to act mad at you because you should have told her and me. So when did this big event happen?"

"A couple of weeks ago."

"And how long have you and Craig been an item?"

"About six months," answered Ella, with a quiet voice.

"Six whole months and you didn't let on once. Why?" Tara rarely raised her voice and the mere fact she did now spoke volumes. She was hurt that Ella hadn't said anything but every time Ella had thought to tell her sister about Craig the words got stuck in her throat.

And that should have been her clue that being with Craig would never work. The *why* she'd been avoiding to answer to both herself and to anyone else was screaming at her. Shrugging, Ella opened the door to the pickup truck. "It's sort of complicated."

Tara opened her car door which happened to be parked adjacent to Ella's truck.

"Ella there's nothing complicated about this. You only get married if you love the guy. So do you?"

No, Ella didn't love Craig, but he'd been the only one in New York who had taken notice of her. The only one she'd even remotely considered and the only man other than Paul she'd had sex with.

"So do you, Ella?"

The urge to cry hit Ella so hard she slumped into the truck. "Oh, Tara what am I going to do?"

Her sister scooted into the truck, pushing Ella over to the passenger side. "It's simple. If you don't love him you have to break off the engagement. It's not like you've told everyone."

"But you don't know Craig."

"Yeah, you got that right. I don't know him. But you can't marry someone you don't love and that's that," declared her younger sister in a motherly voice that stole through Ella. Then Tara gave her a hug and said she'd see her back at the house.

Ella drove on automatic, running through her mind what she'd say to Craig. First things first, she wanted to know how he knew where she was. While they might have been going out for six months she'd been fairly vague about where she grew up. And what right did he have to show up at her house anyway. What's wrong with calling her first? By the time Ella parked her mother's pickup truck in the driveway and made her way up the shoveled driveway thanks to Paul, Ella was in a fine fit.

But the minute her mother opened the door, with a look of absolute rapture on her face, Ella's determination to set matters straight evaporated like melting snow. She allowed her mother to haul her in for a big smothering hug.

"Oh, darling, why didn't you tell us? Never mind. Never mind. I've spent the last two hours with your finance, Craig. He's an absolute delight and so very polite. I was very angry with you for not saying a word but what can I say, except I'm so excited for you. Craig has told me you want to elope but come now, that can't be the case."

"Ah, no, not really," mumbled Ella, letting her mother haul her into the house. And before she could say another word, she was wrapped once again in another set of arms—Craig's. Except her heart didn't once flutter and her knees didn't feel weak like they had when Paul held her.

"I was so worried about you," said Craig, attempting to give her a kiss but at the last moment Ella moved and he ended up giving her cheek a peck instead.

Ella looked at Craig and wished with all her might she felt something. Nothing. Not that Craig at six feet with his wavy blond hair and light brown eyes wasn't a catch, but after being with Paul again she knew going through life without those butterflies was something she couldn't settle for.

"Ah, yeah, how did you find out where my home was?"

Craig chuckled. "Ella my love, it was simple. I called and spoke with your secretary and when she told me you had a car accident well I knew I had to see for myself you were one hundred percent okay and she didn't hesitate to give out your family address."

Ella made a mental note to have a talk with her secretary when she got back...if she got back. For a moment she recalled her afternoon mission and the delight she had discovering that there was real potential for her to start up her own business in town.

"I'm so happy to see you and know that you're okay. You had me really worried," said Craig, a smile lighting up his face.

Why did Ella not believe him? The only thing that usually worried Craig was work and his family. Ella might not know Craig well and had only met his family once briefly but that had been enough. His family had been born with wealth and they wore it like an accessory. She often wondered why Craig worked so hard when he didn't need to prove himself to anyone or pull in the large paycheck he did.

Thinking of that made Ella feel more miserable. "Thanks Craig. Sorry, I guess I should have texted you."

Craig laughed. "Ella my love you are to call me when things like that happen."

Ella nodded, thinking most of their discussions actually did revolve around texting so that had been her automatic thought. Plus, knowing Craig's busy schedule as a public prosecutor he never took a call—it always went to voice mail. Moving into the living room, Ella immediately began stuffing chocolate from the always full candy bowl into her mouth. With her mouth occupied she hoped to avoid talking because speaking meant dealing with the weird situation she found herself in.

"Craig was about to tell me when you two were planning to get married," said her mother with an eager look on her face. A look Ella most certainly did not want to crush.

"Mom, why don't we leave Craig and Ella alone for a while," said Tara, moving the candy bowl out of reach as she winked at Ella.

Ella mouthed a 'thank you' and waited for her mother to refuse but Tara was having none of that. Tara helped her mother up from her chair, telling her she wanted to show her some new designs she was working on. And presto, just like that, Ella was left alone with Craig.

Craig moved closer on the sofa so that their legs brushed against each other. Ella waited for that tingly feeling she experienced with Paul but when nothing happened she realized she had to spit out those hard words now and not later.

"Finally alone. I've been dying to see you." Craig moved closer into Ella in an attempt to claim a kiss. Ella moved out of reach and tried hard not to feel awful when Craig gave her a confused look.

"You're really not happy that I'm here, are you?" he asked, composing himself. "How come you're not wearing your ring?" He tried not to sound accusing and failed.

The ridiculous larger-than-life diamond he'd presented to her two weeks ago still sat in the black velvet box it came in. She hadn't had the courage to tell him the night he'd proposed she hated the massive rock. Most women would die for it but all it did was make Ella feel fake.

"I never thought about it in my dash to get here and no...its okay you're here."

"Don't lie to me Ella. I was worried. What was I supposed to do?"

"Text me."

"I tried," he said, "but you didn't respond."

Damn, she'd forgotten that part of her cell hadn't been working since the accident. "Sorry, my cell sort of got damaged in the car accident."

"And once again you didn't think to call and tell me about that." He tried to sound hurt but it came out more accusing than anything and instantly Ella felt her anger rise.

"You were out of town. I told you I was going to visit with my family over the holidays and you said you would be out of town on business, if I recall."

"Yeah, well I wrapped up the business early and really wanted to see you."

He sidled up closer to her again and Ella fought not to move. Maybe if she let him kiss her she'd feel something. This time when Craig made a move to capture her head to draw her attention to his lips she let him. Like the knee brush though, Ella felt nothing. And without a doubt she now knew that wasn't normal. Less than an hour ago she'd wanted to strip Paul naked and crawl all over his body simply from one kiss.

"What's wrong?" asked Craig, the minute the kiss ended.

She looked into his brown eyes and tried hard to recall why she'd even agreed to be his wife. They were complete opposites. Craig was born in the big city and loved the corporate world. He worked as a public prosecutor following in his father's footsteps and loved the idea of moving into a condo together—not a house, with a backyard and swings for children. His idea of a vacation was to visit another city, not the country. She looked at his slick black business suit and realized she'd never seen him in a pair of jeans. And when they had sex it was planned and meticulous. He insisted she be on the pill and still he used a condom, citing some weird statistical evidence that the pill wasn't a one hundred percent guarantee but with his added protection he all but stated he never wanted children.

"You're looking pale, Ella, are you sure you're okay?" asked Craig.

No, she certainly wasn't okay. "I've got a really bad headache," said Ella.

"I should leave and let you get to sleep."

"I think that might be a good idea, Craig," said Ella, feeling like a heel for not gathering her courage to tell him she didn't want to marry him.

He patted her knee, a gesture he did a lot and one she had always loathed. It felt almost condescending.

"Well, I guess I'll go. I'm staying at the only hotel in town," he said with a forced chuckle. "Why don't I give you a call in the morning?"

Ella stood up to move toward the front porch, which force him to follow her. "Sure, we'll touch base in the morning."

"It's great to see you again," said Craig, bringing her into his arms. Ella simply stood still. When he finally got the hint that she wasn't returning his hug, he let her go.

"Are you sure you're okay?" he asked again.

I'll certainly be better once you leave. "I'm fine. It's just a headache. I'll text you tomorrow."

Silently he buttoned up his fashionable black winter coat and only once the door was open did he turn back to her. He gave her one final kiss on the cheek and then thankfully stepped out the door, leaving Ella the space to finally breathe.

A few minutes later both Tara and her mother returned to the living room. By this time Ella was a wreck. Trying to compose herself, she grabbed two more chocolate candies to plop in her mouth. Even the sugar high wasn't helping.

With a mother's understanding, Ella's mom put on the kettle in the kitchen and then sat down beside her.

"Craig seems like a nice young man, but if he's not the man for you, you have to do the right thing."

"You heard us?" asked Ella, looking at both her sister and mother as she fought the tears.

Both of them nodded.

"Tara told me you were going to end things. Is that really what you want?" asked her mother.

Ella sighed. "I'm not sure. Craig really is a nice guy..."

"Nice. Honey, of course he's nice. You like him. He likes you, but that a marriage won't last," said her mother, rising to answer the shrill whistle from the kettle.

The minute her mother left the room, Tara was on her. "You should have told him. You don't really have a headache, do you?"

"Well, even if I didn't before I do know. This is such a mess."

Tara plopped down beside her and hauled her in for a sisterly hug. "Ella, if you don't love Craig you do need to tell him. Plus, it sure looked to me like things between you and Paul had changed."

Ella felt her cheeks heat. "You saw us?"

"Just enough to know I should not stick my head any further and certainly yell louder," said Tara, chuckling.

"God, this is awful. Paul must think I'm terrible. I can't believe this is happening."

"What's happening?" asked her mother, carrying a tray with three steaming mugs of tea and slices of apple pie with cheese.

O'Connor women always dealt better with weird situations when caffeine and sweets were consumed with gusto.

"Ella and Paul," said Tara, grinning wickedly at Ella.

"Oh, Ella, Paul's never forgotten you but you broke his heart when you left and didn't return."

"Well, it wasn't completely broken, he did get married," stated Ella, sipping her tea, hoping the caffeine would help ease the ache in her mind and heart. She shivered, recalling the feel of Paul's muscles. Gone was the adolescent boy she'd fallen in love with and the man he'd become made her come undone. If her sister hadn't interrupted them she was fairly certain they would have done what they had done all those years before behind the bleachers and just go at it without any inhibitions.

"He only got married when he thought you were never coming back and even that didn't last. Don't get me wrong, I'm thrilled that you and Paul are reconnecting but that boy has grown into one strong, handsome man and he's not to be trifled with."

"Mom, why don't you just say what's on your mind," said Tara, sarcastically.

"Well, if I did that, you'd leave the room running when you should be returning that nice doctor's phone calls," said Gwen, eyeing both her daughters enough to make them squirm under her intense gaze.

"Okay, that's not fair. First off, I've got to deal with Craig," said Ella, taking a bite of the heavenly warm pie her mom had fixed for her. The taste of cinnamon and nutmeg, her mother's special ingredients in her famous apple pies reminded her of Paul. Paul used to play a pie game when she'd sneak pieces to him when they'd meet up at the old hunting shack. One bite of pie for a kiss. It was a memory she'd totally forgotten until this moment and instantly it brought tears to her eyes.

Misunderstanding why she was crying, both her mother and sister hugged her.

"It will be okay, Ella," said her mother.

"Once you end things with Craig," said her sister.

Ella couldn't say anything. She wasn't sure who was correct, but one thing she knew for certain was that she'd blown things with Paul tonight. No way would he want anything to do with her now after learning she'd lied to him.

Paul was one of those stoic men who treasured honesty above all else. Ella knew that more than most people because he'd been lied to for most of his childhood thanks to his drunk father. He'd once told her, after they'd shared a hot intimate moment at the shack, he'd never be like his father, who lied his way through life. Honesty and integrity were part and parcel of Paul's nature. For the first time in her life Ella didn't know how to tackle the situation. Considering she was always the take charge kind of girl, what she'd experienced tonight truly took the wind from her sails.

Chapter Eight

Paul downed the bitter rum and wished with all his might he could get drunk without his conscience screaming that this wasn't him and he wasn't like his deadbeat drunk father.

"Another," said Paul to the bartender, who eyed him long and hard.

"Everything all right?" asked Brody, the bartender who was easily pushing sixty, and who had known Paul since he was a teen trying to sneak into the bar with a fake card.

"Yup, just great," said Paul, downing his fourth double rum and coke.

"Well, that's great, Paul. Last call for food. You want me to order something for you?" said Brody, pushing the greasy menu next to Paul's tumbler.

Paul shook his head. "Nope. I'm good."

"Yeah, that's what you said," said Brody, sighing as he snatched up the menu and turned to pour a drink for the customer at the far end of the counter.

Paul was pleased he was once again alone with his thoughts. Brody could push sometimes and try to loosen his tongue, but tonight Paul suspected his dark attitude was all the warning the bartender needed to back away.

"I'll have what he's having," said Rob to Brody, adding "And a plate of fries."

Brody nodded and then slipped behind the bar to issue the order to the kitchen staff. Paul wasn't in the mood to talk and seriously hoped Rob wanted to be his drinking companion for the night. One look at the man he'd called friend for the past five years and he knew that wasn't to be the case.

"So, what's new?" asked Rob.

Paul turned slightly on the barstool and looked at Rob. "Not much."

"Okay," said Rob, obviously not buying it.

Paul took a sip of his drink, wishing it would erase the memory of holding Ella in his arms. It wasn't working.

"Busy day at the hospital?" asked Paul, not really caring what Rob's answer would be but those damn manners of Mrs. O'Connor's had not only rubbed into his subconscious, they'd dug deep roots inside the man he was now. Pushing aside his drink, Paul turned to study Rob.

"Tara called you, didn't she?"

Rob gave a half smile and his shoulders relaxed. "Guilty as charged. So you want to talk about it?"

"Not really. It's ancient history."

"You sure about that?" said Robert, taking a sip of his drink.

"Doesn't matter what I think. She's bloody well engaged."

Rob swiveled on the bar stool as he turned to look out at the bar crowd. "You sure about that?"

Paul wished he'd ordered ice water. His hands felt idle but he no longer sought the comfort of the alcohol, knowing full well it would only give him a headache, and solve nothing. "Trust me, I'm sure."

"Well, according to Tara, that's not the case for much longer. Guess the guy's nice but he doesn't make Ella's knees go weak."

"What?" Paul wondered what game Rob was playing.

"I'm just repeating what Tara said."

"What the hell does that mean...knees go weak?"

Rob laughed. "Tell me you're not that dense."

Rob gave Paul a long hard look. "Guess you might be. Well, you'll figure it out."

"Are you trying to tell me that she's not going to marry that guy?"

"Looks that way, but she might change her mind," said Rob grabbing his drink.

"What the hell does that mean?"

Rob waited until the fries were set in front of him and then he pushed them toward Paul so they could share. "It means, if I were you, I'd work on my charm and start pursuing what your heart really wants."

"You know Rob, it's a good thing you're a GP because you suck at giving advice."

Rob laughed which made Paul chuckle, and damn if that didn't make him feel marginally better than the drinks he'd downed. "So what's up with you and Tara?"

This time Rob was the one fidgeting. "Not a lot. I'm going to miss this place."

"You going somewhere?"

Rob ate another handful of fries dipped in ketchup before answering. "It's time I moved on."

"Not surprised. You were a city doc first so it always surprised me you decided to stay. If the accident hadn't happened—"

"But it did."

"It wasn't your fault."

"Yeah, heard that enough times over the years. You know Paul it might not have been my fault but in this town it doesn't matter."

Paul had nothing to say to that because Rob was right. Rachel had been one of their own, a bright shining star who'd left at the beginning of September only to return with the beginning of summer with a doctor in tow. A townie, who'd insisted on hitting the waters off the Cape when he'd been warned a storm was coming. If Paul hadn't already been at sea on his way back to port Rob would have drowned like Rachel. But fault wasn't the issue. Rob was an out of towner and while he might do well as a doctor he'd never escape his scarred past in this town.

"So when is this big move of yours happening?" asked Paul.

"Not sure yet. Soon."

"What does Tara think?"

Rob gave a small chuckle but it sounded forced to Paul.

"Paul don't get the wrong impression. There's nothing between Tara and me."

"Well maybe you should heed your own advice, pal," said Paul, dishing out a few twenties. "Time for me to head home. Looks like I've got a busy day tomorrow."

Rob grinned. "Good luck, Paul. I tell you these O'Connor girls aren't easy."

"Thank God. If they were easy do you honestly think we'd be fighting for them?"

"Touché," answered Rob, turning back to the plate of fries to finish them off.

Paul walked out of the bar a hell of a lot better than he had a few hours ago. Rob was right. The O'Connor girls were special and if there was even a slim chance of having Ella in his life again he was going to fight for her.

The next morning Paul sat for a good five minutes in his truck which was parked next to the O'Connor house as he mustered his courage. Deciding it was time to put on his game face, he strode out and knocked on the O'Connors' door. He waited a minute and tried hard not to fidget.

Tara opened the door letting him in. "She's not here."

Paul stepped through the kitchen and the smell of hot chocolate and hot blueberry muffins hit him. "Did she say where she was going?" He hoped to hell she hadn't gone back to the big city and he hadn't wasted his chance.

Tara sighed. "You know, honestly I'm not sure. She said she had a few things she wanted to take care of this morning."

Paul looked down at his boots. "Did she?"

"Paul, she's not going back to the city if that's what you're thinking. I think she's up to something."

That perked up Paul's attention. "Up to something. Like what?"

Tara shrugged her shoulders. "It's a hunch but yesterday she was talking about that old house up the road for sale."

Paul thought for a moment and recalled the old farmhouse up the road. He used to cut the lawn sometimes for Mrs. Beckman and he'd once convinced Ella to join him in the Beckman's hayloft in their old barn. "Are you talking about Mrs. Beckman's house?"

Tara nodded. "Look, I've got to go before Mom comes down and makes me run her errands this morning." As Tara spoke she grabbed her coat and shimmied into her winter boots.

Paul let her pass and walked with her down to the barn. At the barn door, Tara stopped.

"This is my workplace and I've got a few things to do," said Tara, not quite meeting his eyes.

Paul got the hint. Tara had always been shy and secretive about her work and he understood that. "Thanks Tara. I think I'll head over to the old farmhouse and see is she's there."

"I think that's a good idea," said Tara. A second later she slipped through the barn door.

Paul turned back to his truck and within minutes found himself at Mrs. Beckman's farmhouse. The place, like many old farm homesteads in the area, had fallen on hard times. He peeked in through the windows thinking everything looked like it belonged in a museum. The old-fashioned farm stove stood black and solemn in the kitchen with the long wooden table and chairs, a reminder of simpler times. Moving along the edge of the house he walked through the overgrown bush path to the barn and that's when he heard the voices. It was then Paul noticed the fancy SUV parked to the side of the barn which must have come in through the other driveway and Mrs. O'Connor's parked Jeep.

Not sure what to do and feeling like he might be invading a private moment, Paul still trudged up to the barn. The barn door was almost off its hinges and tilted at an odd angle, but it allowed Paul privacy as he eased up to listen in on the conversation. It was then he realized Ella was crying.

To Hell with this. Paul strode in, determined to give the guy his own version of hell for hurting Ella.

"Everything all right in here, Ella?" asked Paul making it clear by his sweep of the guy he wasn't impressed.

"Paul? What are you doing here?" asked Ella, wiping at her tears.

The sight made him furious. Without really thinking he strode forward to ease up to her side. "You okay?"

She nodded her eyes darting back and forth between him and the guy.

"Listen Ella, if this guy's hurt you–"

The guy laughed. "I take it you must be Paul. As hard as this is to believe you've got it all wrong. It's more like Ella's broken my heart, haven't you Sweetheart?"

Paul ground his teeth. He liked the broken heart part but damn he didn't like anyone calling *his* Ella sweetheart.

"Craig and I were just talking and..."

"And she broke up with me," said Craig.

"You did?" asked Paul, trying hard to fight the grin that wanted to escape.

Ella nodded and then kicked at some old dusty hay lining the barn floor. "Craig I just think we worked much better as friends."

Oh, yeah, Paul really liked to hear those words because friends meant this guy would soon be leaving and he'd get Ella all to himself.

Craig moved closer to Ella and Paul tried hard not to step between them. The fact they had a shared history and intimacy wasn't one he wanted to dwell on.

"I'm going to go and if you change your mind—"

"She won't," said Paul.

"Yeah, tell that's her decision and like I said to Ella, where the hell were you all the years she was away?"

Low blow. "For your information Craig, I was here doing what I could to help my community and her mom and sister. I never left."

"This what you want?" asked Craig to Ella.

Ella smiled at Craig. "Yeah, this is what I want. I left but I've come back on my own terms."

Paul edged closer to Ella, making it clear he wasn't the one leaving.

"Well, I'll be going. I wish we'd had this conversation a while ago," said Craig.

"Yeah, me too," said Ella.

Craig looked like he was waiting for a hug or kiss goodbye but Paul was having none of that. Going for the dramatic, he pulled Ella into his arms and said goodbye to Craig for both of them. She stiffened for a moment but the second Craig started to move she melted more into his embrace.

The minute Craig left, Paul turned her into his arms so that they were face to face. The sound of the SUV driving away sounded perfect to Paul.

"Is it true? You're staying?" His heart felt like it was beating like a jackhammer. She eased more into his arms and then smiled up at him, her hazel eyes still red from her tears. "Why were you crying?"

"Paul, until I came here I thought I'd marry Craig."

"And now that you came here?" He tried hard to keep that hopeful note from his voice.

"Everything's changed."

"In a good way," he said, bending his head down to give her a kiss on the lips.

She responded exactly how he loved. Tentative at first but then all woman and all passion. Her hands crept up to his head to finger his hair while his hands crept lower to cup her bottom. The need to kiss her senseless slammed into him and Paul wasn't sure who moved them toward the pile of hay stacked at the back of the barn but the next thing he knew he'd hoisted her onto the stack and was zipping down her winter jacket. Puffs of cold air mingled in the barn with their hot breath as they reluctantly broke the kiss long enough for them to both shrug off their jackets.

Keeping his eyes on her, he moved his attention to undoing her blouse. "You're really staying?"

She looked at him while her nimble fingers undid his own flannel shirt. "Oh yeah, I'm staying."

"And this?" he asked, parting her shirt which revealed a pink lacy bra he couldn't wait to unhook.

She laughed. "This is perfect. Just like I remember, only better."

"I'm not the same man, Ella."

She yanked off his shirt and hauled him into the vee of her legs with her heels "I'm not the same either and I think that's good."

"You've got to know that I've never stopped loving you," he said, meaning it with all his heart.

"They say you never forget your first and it's true. I never forgot you even when I tried to," she said with a sexy sigh.

Paul smiled. "Well, just in case your memory's a little rusty how about I remind you how good we are together." Before Ella could respond Paul leaned his head closer to her chest to lay a path of sweet, light kisses across the tempting swell of flesh exposed by her push-up bra. Then he moved up to her neck, and at her earlobe he kissed her and was instantly rewarded with a girly laugh.

"I think you forgot how much that makes me laugh," she said.

"Trust me, I've forgotten nothing about you," he said, breathing into her ear, watching as goose bumps skimmed to life along the right side of her.

She ran her hands up his back and the feel of those delicate fingers caressing him made him ache all over. His erection pressed against his zipper with an urgency he tried hard to ignore.

"It's broad daylight?" she said, breathless with anticipation. "We really shouldn't be doing this."

With his lips close to hers he said, "Do you remember what we did in the hayloft?"

She blushed. "We almost got caught."

"All I remember was that it was the first time I made you come," he said, grinning as he captured her mouth for a devouring kiss.

When their lungs were both desperate for oxygen they released each other. "I can't tell you how many nights I've thought of that," said Ella, her hands still sliding across his chest.

Paul wanted more than anything to resume their makeout session but he also knew this was his one chance to get it right. "I want to make you come again and again and as much as I'd love to start this moment, you're right. I promise to stop ravishing you if you'll go on a date with me tonight."

She looked up at him and smiled. "I'd love that. I really would." She shivered and Paul was the one who handed her the discarded jacket.

She was cold and tonight he wanted more than a quickie with her, he wanted to love her all night long and heat her on the inside and out.

Cupping her head with his hands, Paul looked at her. "You and me tonight. I'll pick you up at seven. I'm going to leave now because I swear to God if I stay five more minutes we're going to be all over that cold straw because more than anything I've missed you."

She laughed. "I've missed you but you're right. Cold straw and an equally cold barn aren't that inviting. Guess we're not like we used to be when that wouldn't deter us."

He invaded her space again and cupped her head with both hands. "I want you more than I did when I was a teenager but tonight I want it to last. And trust me, knowing I could have you here in this barn is going to leave me hot and hard and taunt me all day."

She gasped and smiled. "You won't be the only one aching."

Ella kissed him then, reminding him once again why he'd fallen head over heels in love with her all those years ago.

Breaking the kiss was hard but getting it right was more important. Paul stepped back from her embrace. "Tonight. Seven. Be ready."

She slid off the pile of hay and plucked some pieces of the dried hay from her hair and jeans. "Oh, I'll be ready."

Paul gave her a quick peck on the cheek and left. More than anything he knew anticipation was going to make this day a killer but if the reward ended up being with Ella forever it would be worth the torture.

Chapter Nine

Ella was on cloud nine. What had started out as one hell of a morning because she knew she had to end things with Craig, had turned into one sweet feeling of anticipation all day. The thought of finally being together with Paul left her feeling like a school girl – giddy and tingly all at the same time. Her hands ached to touch all of his new muscles and the feel of his skin on her fingers had felt wonderful and so right. For a minute she'd been hurt when he'd said let's wait but she knew he was right. This was their one time to get it right and while a quick loving would have been nice in the barn, a long night of having complete access to Paul's muscled-up body would be even better.

"What's got you smiling?" asked her mother, who was as usual mixing up something in the kitchen. For a woman who had a stroke a week ago you'd never know.

"Well, you'll be proud of me. I ended things with Craig."

"And that's why you're smiling?"

"No, Paul sort of came in and...well, I have a date with him tonight."

Her mother stopped mixing and turned on her to pull her in for a hug. Ella didn't even care that she now had flour all over her shirt.

"I'm so happy for you. But are you sure about this?"

"Yeah, I'm sure."

"Don't you go breaking that man's heart, Ella. He's not the kind of guy who'd be happy with a weekend fling."

Ella knew that and she smiled more. "No worries. I'm going to stay."

"Stay? Are you sure?"

"Mom, the other day you were begging me to stay."

Her mother released her. "Honey, of course I want you to stay but if you're happy in New York, I'm happy for you."

"Well, I'm not happy in New York and coming here, being in this small town again, made me realize this."

"So what do you plan to do?" said her mother, pouring a cup of sugar into her mixing bowl.

"At the moment, enjoy my night with Paul."

"What, you've got a date with Paul? So you told Craig to pack his bags?" said Tara, coming into the kitchen like her firecracker self. She had dried bits of pottery all over her, including clumps in her hair. She looked a mess but seemed unusually vibrant.

"Yes I said goodbye to Craig, and yes again I've got a date with Paul. And you look like something blew up all over you."

"I know, but I finally figured out what I was doing wrong with that damn pot."

Tara helped herself to a glass of water and snagged a still-too-hot muffin to eat. "So what are you wearing on your date?"

It was on the tip of Ella's tongue to say she hoped not a whole lot. "Not sure."

"Did you bring anything fancy with you? I figured you'd be the one with all the New York stuff," said her sister, giving her a friendly wink.

Ella hadn't brought much because she knew she wouldn't be partying but that didn't mean she hadn't packed at least one tantalizing black dress. Smiling, she turned to her sister, picked up a second muffin and said, "You know you're right. I've got the perfect outfit for tonight." Then it dawned on her. She'd brought the dress but lacked the boots. "Would you have a pair of sexy boots I could borrow?"

"Good thing we're both the same size. I've got the perfect boots for you. Just wait until you see them, you'll love them."

Giddy with what she was about to do tonight, Ella didn't quite know how to spend the rest of her day. She'd been anxious all morning, trying to find the perfect words to end her relationship with Craig but with that out of the way, and with it having gone a lot better than she'd anticipated, she still had more than six hours to kill.

Her sister pulled her arm. "You and I are going somewhere."

"Where?" asked Ella. Her sister's idea of a good time often left Ella feeling left out. It wasn't so much the years separating them but their personalities. The last time Ella had made her go out for a fun night they'd spent two hours firing at each other in a sport called paintball which Ella had hated.

"You are not to say another word until we get there and if you do," said Tara with a devilish grin on her face, "then you won't be getting my sexy boots."

"That's blackmail."

Tara laughed. "Yeah, I know. Maybe I should have been the lawyer in the family."

Ella smiled as she let her sister drag her upstairs. "Well, I'm game but you can't go anywhere until you get that stuff out of your hair."

Her sister automatically stopped on the stair and started to yank at the dried mud in her hair. "You know what? The place we're going will take care of that."

Now that more than anything had Ella questioning agreeing to her sister's plan.

Paul was more nervous than the time he'd picked up Ella for their high school prom. Back then the suit he'd borrowed from a friend had been too big. It had actually been Ella's mom who had hemmed the pants after discovering him in their barn one day after school trying to do the job himself. He remembered feeling embarrassed and ashamed. Ashamed his father wouldn't get him his own suit and too damn proud to ask for help. All that Ella's mother had said was she'd like to hem them to make sure they were done right. Then with her usual tact she'd asked if he'd do her a favor and pile the load of wood that needed to be stacked by the back door. That had been her way. He knew it now. She had used her motherly wisdom when faced with an obvious red-faced teenager who had wanted to look handsome and polished the night he'd come to pick up her daughter for their high school dance.

Paul realized he probably should have told Ella his plans but there was a part of him, that old romantic part that had wielded itself to his heart when he'd first met Ella, wanting to surprise her.

Knocking softly on the door, he wasn't surprised when Gwen it.

"My, don't you look handsome," said Ella's mom, urging him inside, with a wide smile.

"Thank you," he said, fighting the urge to blush. *For God's sake, get a grip. You're not a kid anymore.*

"Just you wait until you see Ella," said Gwen, but she didn't have to say another word.

Walking down the stairs, Ella quite literally took his breath away. She wore an off the shoulder slinky black dress that outlined all her curves and sexy black boots that reached all the way up to her knees. No necklace adorned her graceful neck but a pair of tiny diamond earrings dangled from her ears.

"You look amazing," he said.

"Thank you," she said.

Paul took great delight when she blushed. The two of them were acting like love-sick teenagers and that helped the knot of anxiety that had been growing ever since he'd left her this morning. Half of him had thought he was stupid for not going all the way while the other half worried giving Ella time to herself would give her time to second guess her plans. And more than anything Paul wanted to be part of her plans.

Ella fastened up her long black winter dress jacket.

"Shall we?" he said, offering her his arm.

She nodded.

"We'll keep the porch light on but feel free to stay out all night," called Tara from the kitchen, which immediately elicited a huge blush from Ella.

"Just ignore her. She's trying to get me riled."

"Personally, I like her advice," said Paul, as he helped Ella into his truck.

Tucked safely inside his truck, Paul started down the road. They talked about a lot of silly things. How Mrs. Beckman's house shouldn't have been allowed to fall to rot, how Main Street seemed to be making a comeback, and when they passed said street she turned to him and asked where they were going.

"It's a surprise," said Paul, hoping like hell he wasn't making a mistake.

Ten minutes later they turned onto a familiar dirt road which Paul kept plowed all winter.

"Paul, are we really going to your hunting shack?"

"Would you be disappointed if I said yes?"

She leaned closer to him in the truck, "No way. I'd love it."

"You sure, because if you really want to go to a fancy restaurant I also happened to make reservations in town at one, just in case."

She laughed. The sound travelled straight to Paul's heart.

"Don't be silly. You know me. I'd rather it was only you and me anytime."

Paul glanced her way and a minute later took the right in the road. A second later he heard her gasp.

"That is not your shack."

He grinned. "Oh, part of the shack is still there but over the years I've sort of made this place my home." A home away from his ex. He thought that but didn't want to say it, fearing to ruin the mood.

"You did this to keep away from her, didn't you?"

And that's exactly why Ella and he were perfect. She totally got him. "Yeah."

"Did you ever bring her to the shack?"

There was hesitation in Ella's voice and he knew why. The old hunting cabin, really more a shack in the woods, had been their place. The place they'd had solely to themselves to get to know one another. Their first time making love had been on an old worn cot and while the experience had been wonderful that cot certainly hadn't been.

Paul parked the truck. "I brought her up here once and she took one look at the shack and demanded that I turn around and take her back into town. I think we had our first big fight that day."

Ella grinned and then like she realized she probably shouldn't, she bit her lower lip. "Sorry. I know I shouldn't be happy that you didn't bring her here but I sort of thought of this place as our spot."

He leaned closer and hauled her to him, needing to feel the softness of her lips. "And that's exactly what I thought. This place has nothing but happy memories for me. I hope you don't mind coming here with me tonight."

She leaned in and before he could say another thing kissed him. Hesitant at first, they quickly learned the feel of each other's lips. Ella was the one who pulled away. "Thank you for that."

"For kissing you. Any time, darlin'," he said trying to haul her closer for another kiss.

This time Ella leaned away from him. "I want you to show me around this magnificent shack of yours."

Paul grinned. More than anything he wanted to show Ella around his place. Getting out of the truck and helping her to the door, he swept her up into her arms as she squealed in delight. She was light and giggled as he stepped over the threshold with her.

"You're only supposed to do that when you get married," she said.

He gently settled her on her feet. "You, Ella, are the only one I've ever done that to. In my heart we are married."

She looked down at her boots and Paul worried for a second he was pushing things too fast. When she looked up at him, her eyes were glassy.

"Shit, I probably shouldn't have said that," he said.

She moved closer and touched his face. "Paul it took me leaving to realize everything I ever wanted I had here, right at home, with you. You are my one and only."

Paul's heartbeat sped up. He kicked the door shut behind him and pulled Ella into his arms. This time their kiss was like a slow burn, sensually hot and steady. Together they shucked off their jackets, not caring where they fell. Paul backed them up until they bumped into the edge of the kitchen table.

Ella slowly released her hold on him and turned her head. "Did you make all this for us?"

Now Paul was the hesitant one. "Yeah. I sort of wanted to cook for you."

"That has to be the sweetest thing any man could say."

Laughing, Paul moved them into the kitchen as he started adding the condiments to the table. "Well, you might think that but you haven't tried my cooking yet."

She grabbed him around his middle, pulling him in for a hug. "Doesn't matter. The mere fact that you made it means I will love it."

It took a lot of willpower for Paul to finish the meal when all he could think about was peeling Ella out of that damn sexy dress she wore. He let her pick the wine and once they were seated they settled in with small talk. It was an easy conversation. Ella wanted to know all about the changes that were taking place along Main Street and he eagerly filled her in. He told her about his plans for an expansion and realized when she slowly but steadily grilled him she was using her lawyer smarts to give him some very sound advice. It was the type of conversation he'd always wanted to have in a partner. The type of talk that made a man relax after a long hard day. Ella was elegant and poised, praising him countless times for his cooking skills and genuinely impressed with his carpentry. After their second glass of wine, Paul brought Ella from the kitchen into the large living room.

He turned on the music and pulled her in for a slow dance. "Remember this?"

She tilted her head up to look at him, her eyes looked seductive and she felt as sexy as hell in his arms. The sensual music of Neil Diamond's song, *Play Me*, transported them both back to another time when they were young and thought they'd make all the right choices. More than a decade had passed and Paul more than anything wanted to ensure the rest of their time was spent together.

Ella gently kissed him and then said, "I've never forgotten. It's our song. You bribed the DJ at our prom to play it. How could I ever forget?"

"I love holding you, Ella," said Paul, who was letting his hands get reacquainted with the woman in his arms who felt like she belonged there.

"I don't want to rush you but there's one room I haven't shown you yet," said Paul, taking her hand and leading her up a floor to his bedroom.

"I seriously hope it's that bedroom of yours."

Paul laughed. The old Ella would never been brave enough to say that or state her demands and it was with knowing how much she'd changed that his grin grew. The times they'd made love she'd been quiet by necessity and circumstances but Paul planned to ensure he made her roar.

With nervous butterflies in his own stomach, and remembering the first time he'd led her to the shack's bedroom, anticipation coiled hot and thick through his blood. A lot had changed but some things remained the same. Her hands felt the same, tiny and dainty in his and he loved that. The shack had been transformed into a two-storey log cabin equipped with a large stone fireplace and a master suite upstairs that had a large double-bowed window custom-fitted to provide the best sunlight in the place. But more than that – they'd changed. Ella was still that driven girl he'd fallen in love with but over the years shyness had turned into a sexy walk and swagger that had him all but tripping over his feet. And he'd changed, both physically and mentally. He was a take charge kind of guy who'd started with nothing and worked hard to get where he was. He knew what he wanted and went after it. Want he wanted more than anything was Ella sprawled naked in his bed for the entire night.

"Paul, this place is amazing."

"Thanks, I did a lot of it myself."

"I always knew you were a man good with his hands but seriously, this place belongs in a magazine."

"Nope. No magazine. The last thing I want is for my ex to realize what I've done to this place."

"I thought you two were divorced."

"Oh, trust me we are and more than anything I want nothing to do with her again. Ella, you have to know the only reason I married her –"

"Shh, you don't have to tell me your reasons."

He pulled her into the bedroom and she gasped at the large King-sized bed. "Yeah, I do. When you left I thought you'd come back but after the years when you didn't and when I thought I had to get on with my life, Debbie entered it. I know now she was after me for my money. I married her because she said she was pregnant."

"Oh, Paul, I'm so sorry."

"I'm not. More than anything I feel like the lucky one who got away. I'm not even sure she really was expecting but about three months into our marriage she said she'd miscarried and things sort of went downhill fast."

"The only reason I even said yes to Craig was because like you I thought I should try to get on with my life. That's a sad reason."

Paul did not like hearing that man's name on Ella's lips. "Guess we both made some big mistakes."

Ella sat on his bed and patted the spot next to her. "I think the mistakes helped to make us the people we are today."

"And who exactly are we?"

"We are the two people who fell hopelessly in love years ago and tonight it's all about rekindling that love."

Paul didn't sit on the bed. He knelt between her legs and leaned his body into her, kissing her with everything he had.

"From the first moment I saw you I loved you," he said, whispering the words into her ear watching as the familiar goose bumps skimmed to life along her exposed shoulder blade.

"We were five when we met in elementary school. You did not love me then. I recall in fact you pushing me in the mud countless times."

Paul laughed. "That's a five-year-old boy's version of love, Ella."

He reclaimed her lips and loved how her hands settled on his back. When they broke for a breath, she said, "Leaving you was the hardest thing I did but I'm so glad I came back to where I belong."

"And where exactly is that, Ella?"

Ella captured his face in her hands. "Wherever you are, Paul. Wherever you are."

She kissed him then like a woman who knew what she wanted. Quickly they became a familiar mess of tangled limbs as they shimmied more fully onto the bed. Paul kicked off his shoes, and then slowly unzipped Ella's sexy boots. She unhooked the buttons on his dress shirt so slowly he thought he'd go insane. Paul was about to help her out of her dress but Ella had him beat. She whipped the dress over her head and this time Paul was the one gasping.

"Sweet Jesus, where did you get that?"

Ella laughed and lazily drew her arms up over her head. "You like?"

"Oh my God, you are seriously going to kill me."

"This is a gift from Tara. We went into this store to the right of Main Street called the Sex Kitten."

"My new favorite store," said Paul, loving the sexy outfit his Ella was wearing. The hot pink strapless push-up bra and the sexy pink thong had him all but panting with need.

"Remind me to thank you sister."

"How about thanking me, Mr."

"Oh darlin', I'll be thanking you all night."

Lying beside her, Paul trailed light kisses down her neck. "You sure about this Ella?"

Her fingers flew to his belt buckle. If that wasn't an affirmative, he was an idiot. Still though, he needed her to understand he wanted more than a one-night stand. He wanted her in his life for good...forever, till death do you part, which considering how horrible his first marriage was surprised him.

"Ella, will you marry me?"

She laughed. "That's supposed to come after we date, or at least after the dessert part."

He leaned on one elbow to look down at her. Her skin was flushed from their already heated make-out session but she looked up at him with those hazel eyes of hers he knew to the depth of his soul. "I don't want to waste the rest of my life. Too much time has gone already without you in my life." *God, maybe I am pushing things too quickly.*

She captured his lips. "Yes. Yes, Paul. More than anything I want to be with you and in your life."

His heart constricted. He knew she liked living in New York but he wasn't a big city kind of guy. "That means here. In this small town. I can't move to New York and after all you've gone through to make it there you probably should think long and hard about what I'm asking."

"You know what? I never really did fit in with that New York life. This place sounds like the perfect place for our home," she said, her nimble fingers made quick work of his belt buckle.

In seconds they were both naked and laughing, giddy with the joy of each other. This time Paul knew that feeling was going to last not only all night but the rest of their lives. When they got hot and sweaty and both collapsed from round one of their love making, Paul knew with his heart and soul this time was the correct time.

"I'm so glad I came home this Christmas," said Ella, her hand playing with the hairs on his chest.

"That makes two of us," he said.

Finally the shack had become home as they both embraced their future.

I am a proud Canadian but my hubby is part-American and the summer retreats with our children to visit relatives in Cape Cod, Maine, Boston and New Hampshire left a lasting impression. Embrace is a sweet romance but I also write paranormal romance, erotic romance, young adult realistic teen stories (under the pen name Renee Pace) and coming soon a New Adult (yes I write a variety of genres).

I call Halifax, Nova Scotia home and am a true believer in soul-mates. I love being an Indie author and value any feedback. My website is www.reneefield.com[1]. I'm a member or Romance Writers' of America and my local Romance Writers' of Atlantic Canada, the Writer's Federation of Nova Scotia and when not writing I'm managing my on-line company which promotes authors with readers – www.StoryFinds.com[2]

I can be reached by email at renee@reneefield.com.

---

1.   http://www.reneefield.com

2.   http://www.StoryFinds.com

Don't miss out!

Visit the website below and you can sign up to receive emails whenever Renee Field publishes a new book. There's no charge and no obligation.

https://books2read.com/r/B-A-HRN-LKZB

BOOKS 2 READ

Connecting independent readers to independent writers.

Did you love *Embrace*? Then you should read *Electrify Me*[3] by Renee Field!

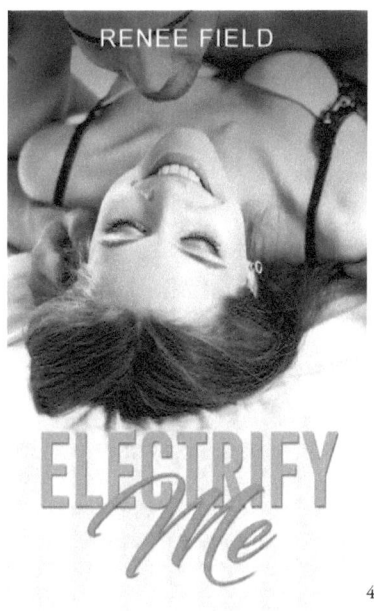

[4]

Krista lives out her fantasies through her vixen-like characters she writes about for her romance publisher. They're sexy, brazen and experienced in and out of the bedroom. When a young hunk of an electrician shows up at her house and offers her a delicious deal that will spark all her creative juices, Krista decides to throw caution out the window. After all she's not getting any younger and the idea of finally becoming a sultry, sexually self-confident woman is a fantasy come true.

Read more at www.reneefield.com.

---

3. https://books2read.com/u/4EDqBz

4. https://books2read.com/u/4EDqBz

Also by Renee Field

A Warriors of Maida Novella
Love Me Wild
Love Me Tender
Love Me Strong
Love Me Wild

Darklander Lovers
Be My Warlock Tonight
Be My Vampire Tonight
Be My Werecat Tonight

Elemental Love
Heart of Mine

Riverton Cove series
Embrace

Titan series
Rapture
Bliss

Standalone
Claiming A Siren's Heart
Claiming Poseidon's Heart
A Siren's Wish
Fairy Cursed
Summer Heat
Queen of Dragons
Summer Heat
Electrify Me

Watch for more at www.reneefield.com.

About the Author

Renee loves to write a variety of genres. She writes for HQN Spice Briefs and also writes sensual paranormal romance, and contemporary romance as an Indie author. Field also writes nitty gritty young adult and paranormal young adult romance novels under the pen name Renee Pace. Renee calls Halifax, Nova Scotia, Canada home and loves her view of the Atlantic Ocean. She is a member of Romance Writers' of America, and her local Romance Writers of Atlantic Canada. She juggles work, four children and is a firm believer in soul-mates and the power of the sea.

Renee loves to hear from fans. She can be reached by email at reneefieldauthor@gmail.com

Read more at www.reneefield.com.